At the Playg

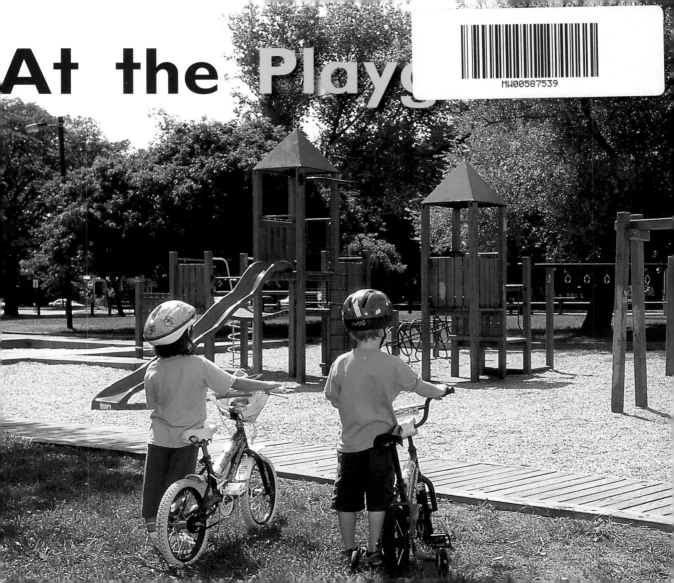

We are going

on the swings.

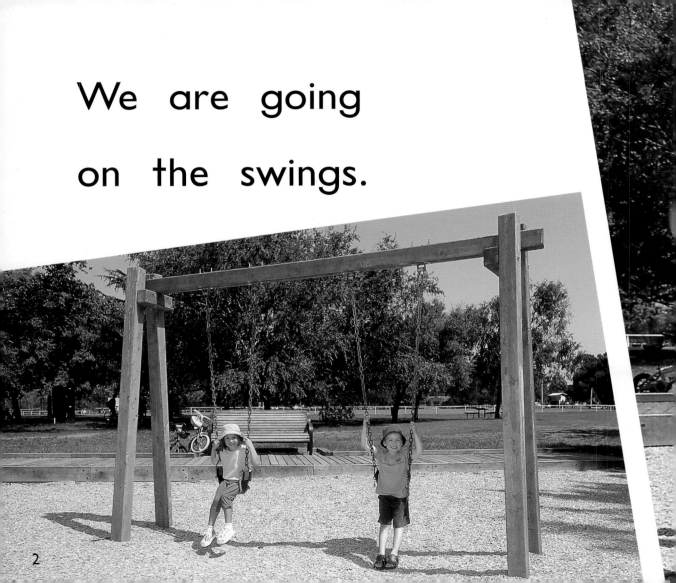

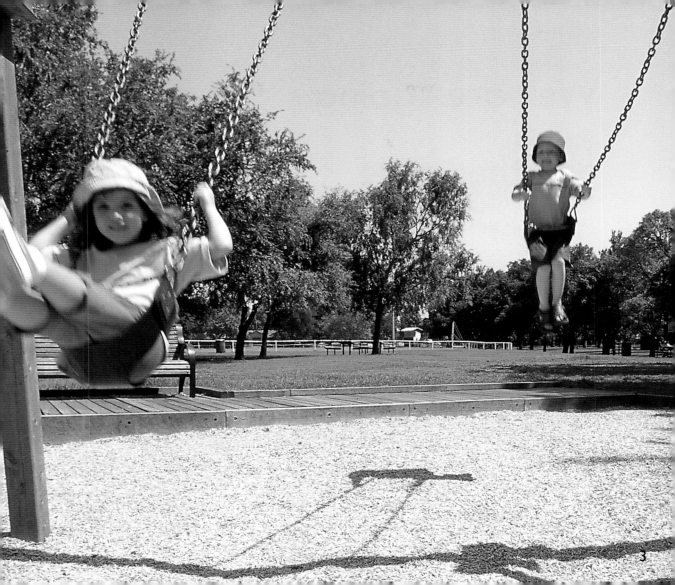

We are going
on the slide.

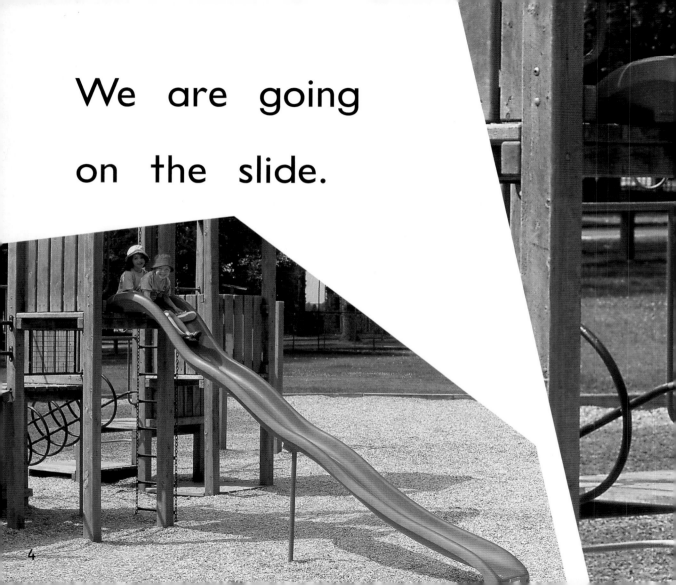

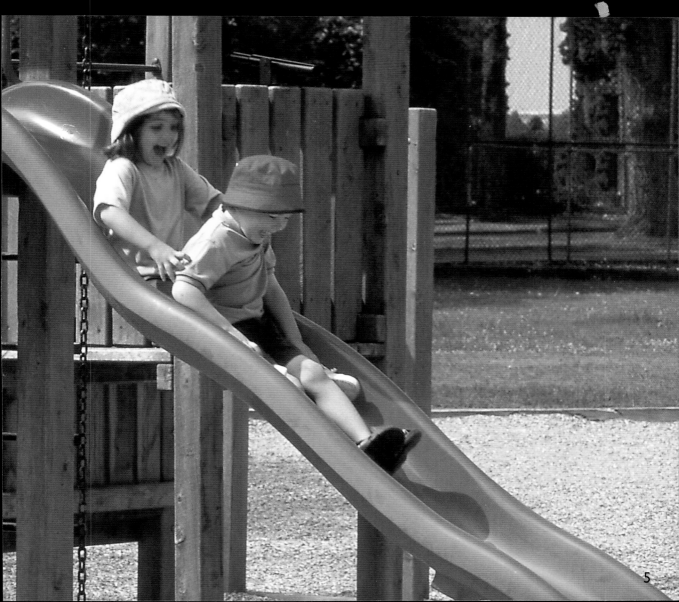

We are going

on the ladder.

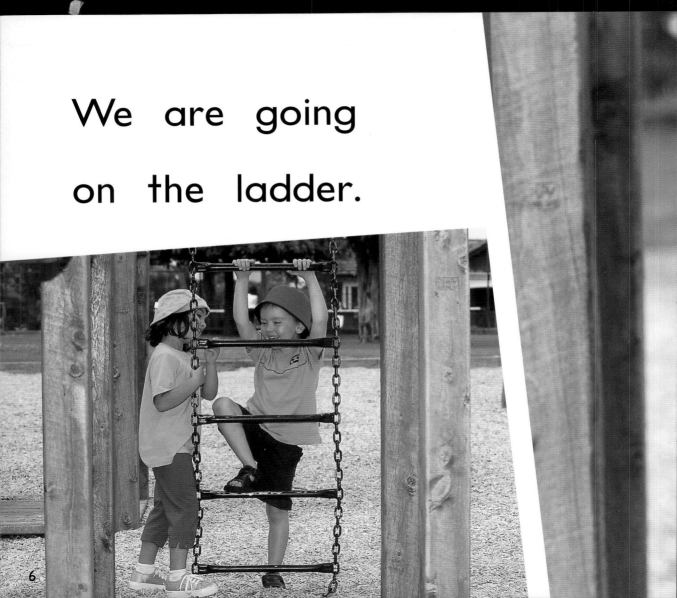

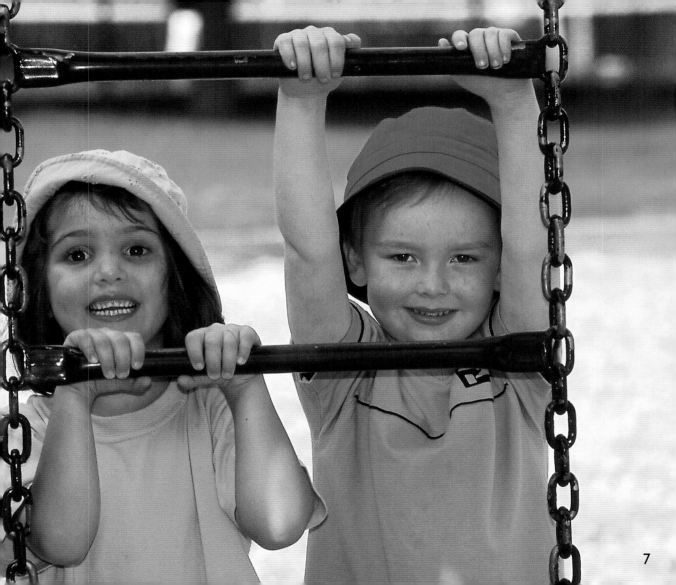

We are going

on the seesaw.

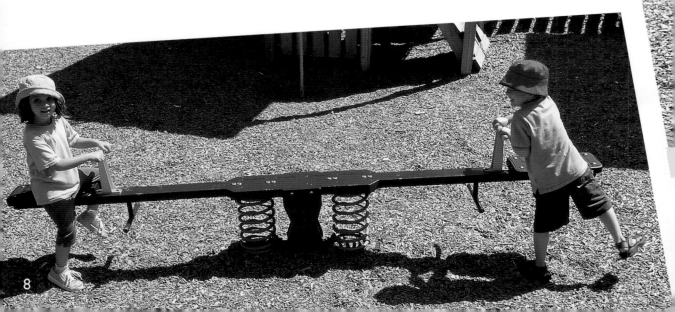

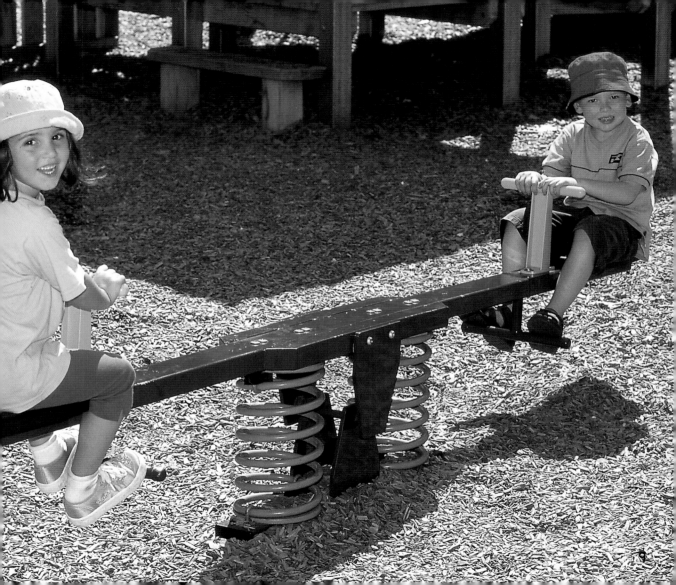

We are going

on the horses.

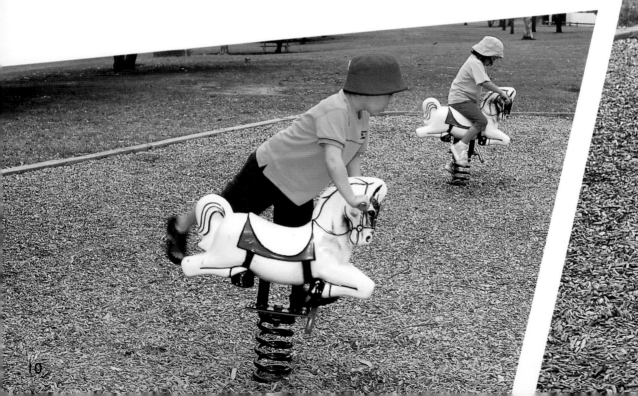

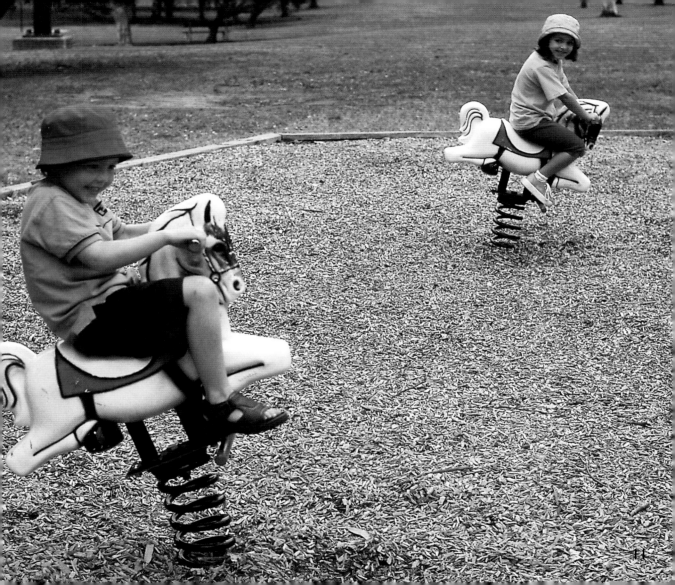

We are going

on the bar.

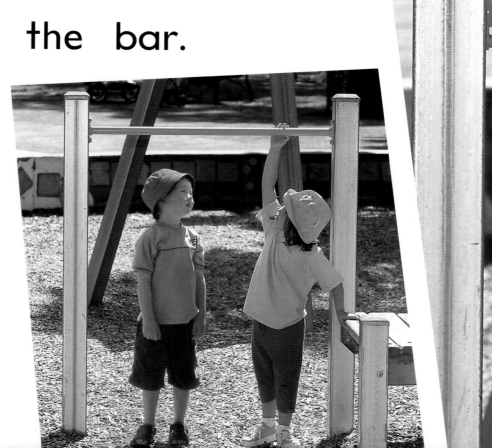

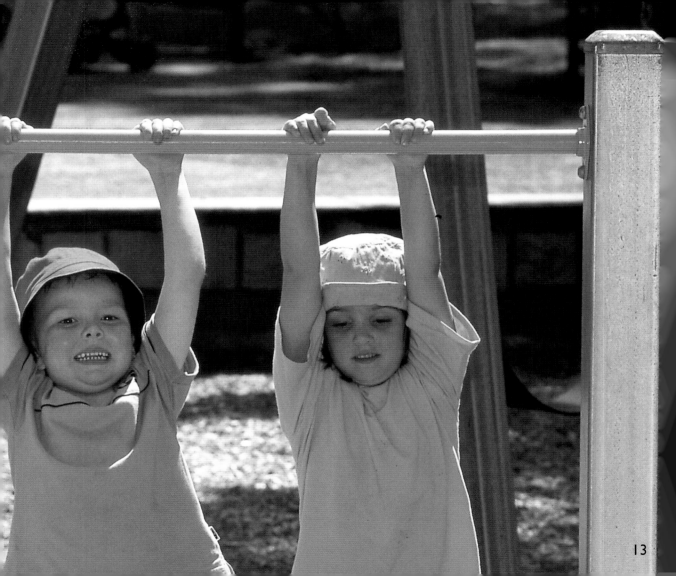

We are going

on the bridge.

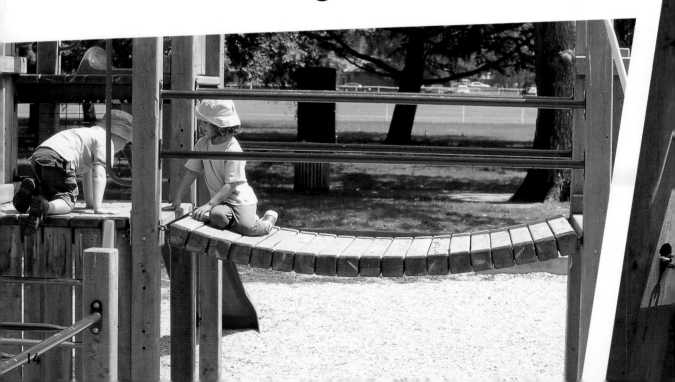

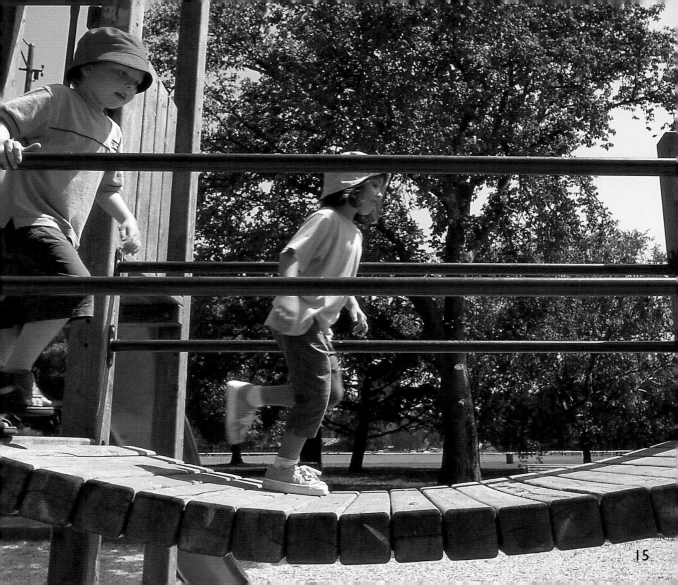

We are going

on the bikes.

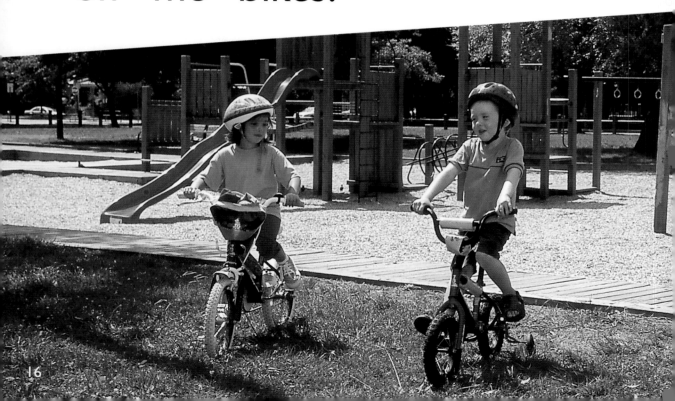